# My Heart Is Like a
# ZOO

## Michael Hall

GREENWILLOW BOOKS

*An Imprint of HarperCollinsPublishers*

My heart is
like a zoo—

eager
as a
beaver,

steady
as a yak,

hopeful as a hungry heron
fishing for a snack . . .

silly
as a
seal,

rugged
as a
moose,

happy as a herd of hippos
drinking apple juice.

Snappy
as a
crab,

angry

as a

bear,

bothered as a bull
with a hornet in its hair.

Cool
as a
penguin,

crafty
as a
fox,

quiet as a caterpillar
wearing knitted socks.

Frightened
as a
rabbit,

jumpy
as a
frog,

gloomy as a lone coyote walking in the fog.

Brave
as a
lion,

thoughtful
as an
owl,

peaceful as a portly walrus
lounging on a towel.

Cozy
as a
clam,

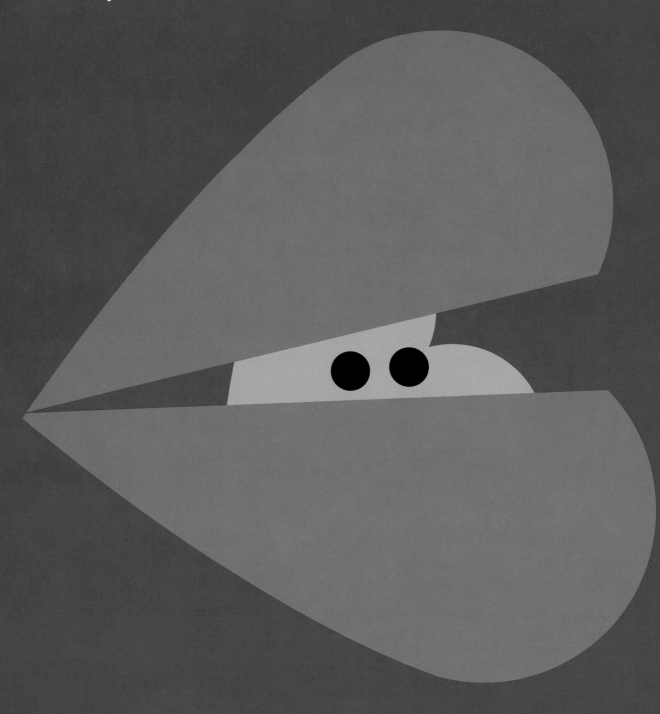

chatty
as a
jay,

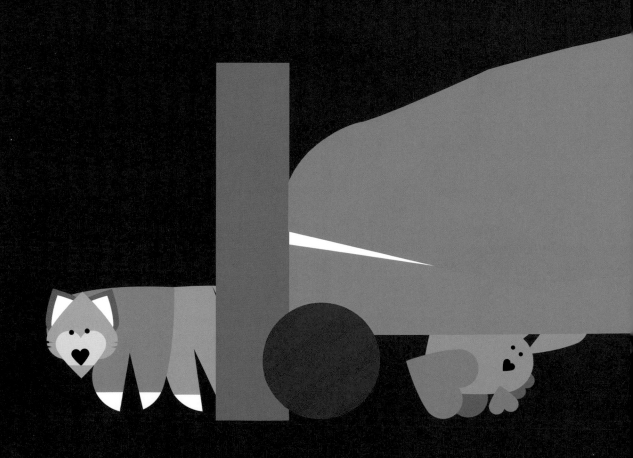

tired as a
zookeeper
who's had
a busy day.

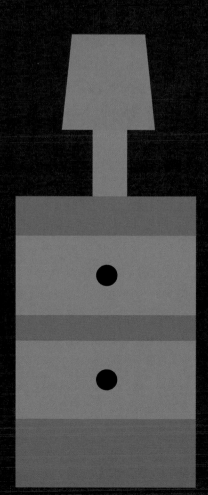

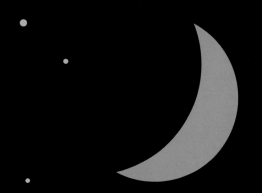

My Heart Is Like a Zoo

Copyright © 2010 by Michael Hall

All rights reserved. Manufactured in China.
For information address
HarperCollins Children's Books,
a division of HarperCollins Publishers,
10 East 53rd Street, New York, NY 10022.
www.harpercollinschildrens.com

Digital art was used
to prepare the full-color art.

The text type is 30-point
Avenir 65 Medium.

Library of Congress Cataloging-in-Publication Data
Hall, Michael, (date).
My heart is like a zoo / by Michael Hall.
  p. cm.
"Greenwillow Books."
Summary: Depicts in rhyming text how love can be many
different things, such as eager as a beaver, steady as a yak,
or silly as a seal.
ISBN 978-0-06-191510-9 (trade bdg.)
ISBN 978-0-06-191511-6 (lib. bdg.)
[1. Stories in rhyme. 2. Love—Fiction.
3. Zoo animals—Fiction.] I. Title.
PZ8.3.H1483My 2010    [E]—dc22    2009017818

10  11  12  13  LEO First Edition 10  9  8  7  6  5  4  3  2  1

Greenwillow Books